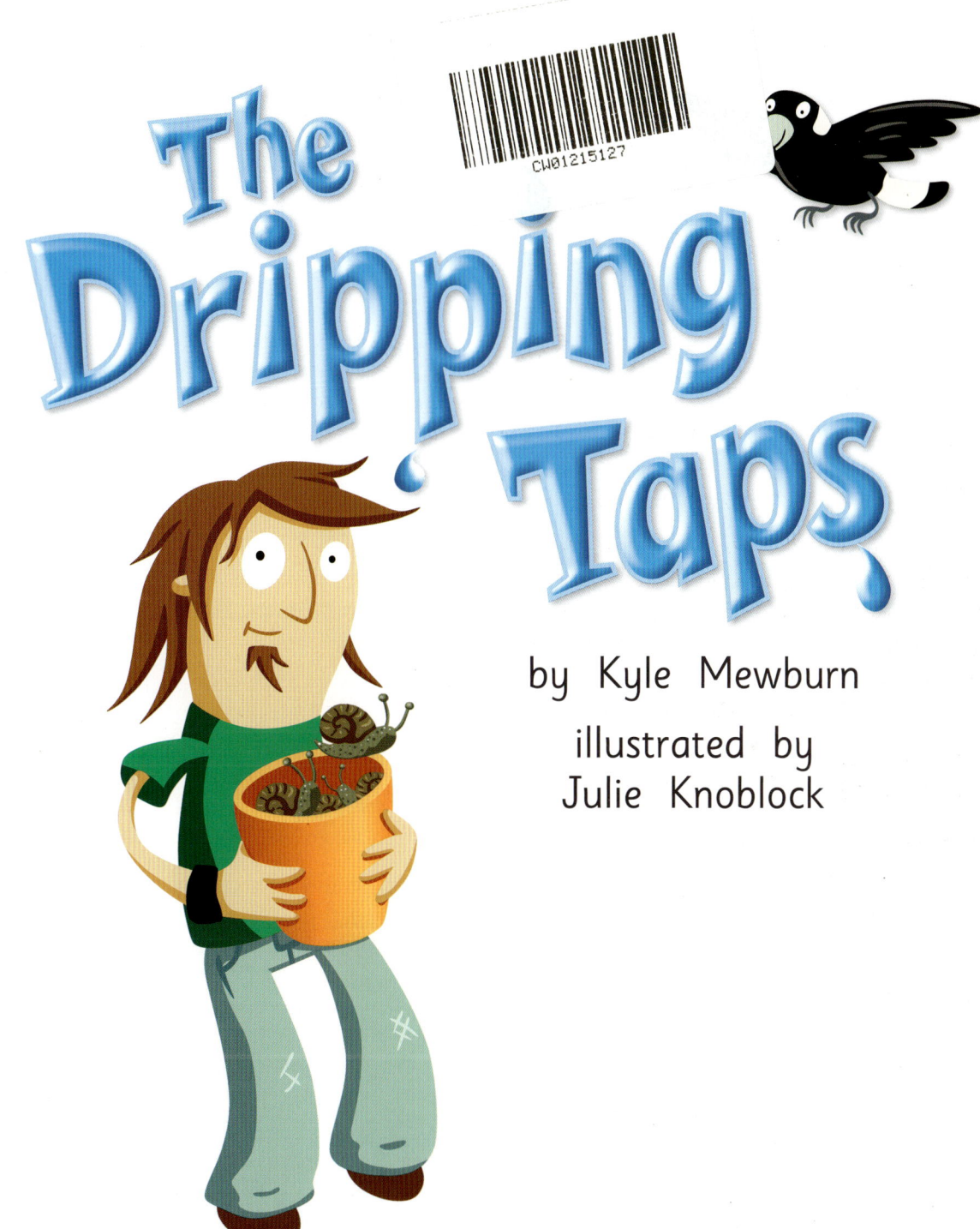

The Dripping Taps

by Kyle Mewburn

illustrated by Julie Knoblock

When Jack had a shower,
the water went on his lemon trees.
The lemon trees liked the soapy water.

Jack didn't like wasting water.
But he did like lemonade.

Some plants don't like soapy water.
So Jack pumped fresh water
up from the creek, too.

But one day there was no water.

"The creek is nearly dry!" said Jack.
"There must be a big leak somewhere."

Jack didn't see any big leaks. All he heard was, *Drip! Drop!* "Let's go, Maggie!" said Jack.

Jack and Maggie followed the river into town.

There were dripping taps everywhere! "Dripping taps waste a lot of water," said Jack. "If we don't stop them, there won't be any water left!"

"This jelly will fix it!" said Jack.

The drips stopped. Jack was happy.

Nobody else was happy!
Soon there was jelly everywhere.
It was on people's noses
and in people's hair.

"I've got a better idea," said Jack.

"Snails like water. They'll be happy to stop the drips," said Jack. "Sometimes snails are faster than people."

"Now there's enough water for everyone," said Jack.